Tara and the Talking Kitten Meet Angels and Fairies

This book is dedicated to my grandchildren
Isabel, Finn, Kailani and Maya
and children everywhere who love kittens.

Text © Diana Cooper 2011
Edited by Elaine Wood
Illustrations © Kate Shannon 2011
Interior design by Thierry Bogliolo

ISBN 978-1-84409-551-3

Printed in the European Union

Published by
Findhorn Press
117–121 High Street
Forres IV36 1PA
Scotland, UK

www.findhornpress.com

Tara and
the Talking Kitten
Meet Angels and Fairies

by Diana Cooper
illustrated by Kate Shannon

FINDHORN PRESS

Parents' and teachers' note

In Tara, Ash-ting and the Angels, *we explore how children can handle difficult situations and unwelcome attention. The children are encouraged to speak to an adult. This is a sensitive but important subject and you may like to read this book with your child and discuss the issues with them. Tara also learns about angels and how to ask for their help.*

Discussions points and exercices for children are available on relevant page of publisher website www.findhornpress.com

Diana Cooper is well known for her books on angels, fairies, unicorns and the spiritual world, all written from her own personal experiences. For more information about these subjects see her website www.dianacooper.com *– there is also a children's corner.*

If you wish to talk to someone about the subjects in this book, the Diana Cooper School website lists teachers throughout the world: www.dianacooperschool.com

Tara, Ash-ting and the Angels

"Tara's reading is very poor," Mum said to Dad in a worried voice. "She's way behind the others in her class."

"She's only seven," replied Dad.

"Yes, but her teacher says she's slightly dyslexic and she gets extra help already. Now she's got to do extra reading practice every day after school," Mum sighed, "as if I don't have enough to do already."

Tara looked miserable. She tried explaining how the letters muddled themselves up, but no-one really understood, so she stopped telling them. The only one who understood and believed her was Ash-ting, her beautiful grey kitten. No one knew their secret. They could talk to each other. She told him everything, even

how the words on the pages sometimes laughed at her, or waved to her.

Ash-ting agreed that it was much more fun to be outside watching the flowers grow and the butterflies flitting from flower to flower.

So Tara sat for a long, horrible time struggling to read a book while Mum tried to be patient with her. But it was clear to Tara that she must be bad because Mum was cross with her. At last the reading was over for the day – but then something worse happened...

At tea time Dad announced that Uncle Steve was coming to stay for a whole week. He was an old school friend of Dad's (not a real uncle), but they had always called him Uncle. Tara groaned, "Oh no," and her mother told her not to be rude.

Mel, her older sister, said she suddenly felt sick and couldn't eat any more food.

Dad did not seem to notice that Tara and Mel disliked Uncle Steve. He said they could all go to a football match together. Mum said he could babysit while she and Dad went out.

Uncle Steve

Uncle Steve arrived the next day. He looked scruffy, had light blue eyes and was going bald. He cracked jokes all the time but the children did not find them funny. Tara did not know why she didn't like him, but she knew she didn't. Ash-ting rubbed up against Tara's leg and whispered, *"Keep out of his way."* Tara nodded. When Mum was in the kitchen with Mel and Jack she went into the sitting room with Ash-ting to watch television. Ten minutes later Uncle Steve came into the room and shut the door behind him.

"Hello Tara," he smiled and sat next to her on the sofa. "My you have grown." He reached over and picked her up, placing her on his knee. She wanted to get off. "You are a pretty little thing," he murmured in a strange soft voice.

Ash-ting did not like this man or how he was being with Tara. *"Tara call for your Mummy,"* he urged, but she felt frozen. She couldn't move and she couldn't speak.

Uncle Steve bounced her up and down on his knee. Tara felt uncomfortable. She didn't like sitting on his lap. He had his arms round her like Daddy did but it didn't feel the same – she just didn't like it. She didn't like him.

Suddenly the little tiny fluffy grey kitten decided to act. He leapt onto the sofa and dug his claws into Uncle Steve's face. The man threw Tara off his knee and cursed. He picked the brave little kitten up by the scruff of its neck and marched through the house with him, throwing him roughly out of the back door into the garden.

"Whatever's the matter?" cried Mum. Uncle Steve told her the kitten had scratched his face.

"I'm so sorry," said Mum. "But why would he do that? He's always so gentle."

Uncle Steve lied in reply and said he had accidentally trodden on the animal's tail. He gave Tara a threatening look and she shrank away.

As soon as she could she rushed out of the open door into the garden and picked up Ash-ting. "Thank you," she sobbed. "Oh you poor brave thing, are you hurt?"

"I'm alright," said the kitten, as he continued to groom his ruffled fur. *"But Tara you must tell an adult what happened."*

Tara went and stood by her Mummy in the kitchen and tried to tell her, but the words wouldn't come out of her mouth. And what was there to tell? He only hugged her. But she knew it felt wrong and he did lie about treading on Ash-ting's tail.

Tara's Drawing

Next day in school they had to draw a picture of the people who live in their house. Tara's friend Rosy drew herself and her Mum. Tara included Uncle Steve in her picture. She drew him big and black with a big red hand reaching out like Mr. Tickle and going round her. Mummy and Mel were pink and Daddy, Jack and she were coloured blue. Tara took a long time over her picture.

After school Tara stuck to Mummy like glue. For a change Mel did, too. The two girls were very helpful indeed. Mummy told them that she and Daddy were going to have a meal at Tracy's parents' house later and Uncle Steve was going to look after them for the evening. Tracy was in Tara's class and lived just a few doors away.

The children protested, but Mummy just laughed. "You'll be fine with Uncle Steve."

Dad gave Mel his mobile. "You only have to call Mummy's number if you need us," he said.

The children were all in bed when Mum and Dad went out. Tara felt unhappy and scared. Life was horrible. First she couldn't read properly so Mummy was grumpy. Now Uncle Steve was here. She couldn't bear it. Nothing ever went right and she felt no one loved her. She felt very sad.

Tara heard Uncle Steve's footsteps on the stairs and she held her breath. But he passed her door and went to the bathroom. She felt afraid, but wasn't sure why. She held Ash-ting tight and whispered, "Help! Oh help!"

Tara's Angel

Suddenly a glowing golden light started to build in the corner of Tara's bedroom. It was bright and glorious and warm. Tara and Ash-ting sat bolt upright in bed; they could scarcely believe their eyes. It was an angel.

A gentle voice said, "Hello Tara. I'm your guardian angel and I'm always with you. I love you very much. I love you whether you can read well or not. I love you and I'm here to help you. Now I want you to get up immediately and go into Mel's room."

Tara did not need to be told twice. Clutching Ash-ting, she rushed out of the room and into her sister's bedroom, where she jumped into bed and held onto Mel. Strangely, Mel did not protest; she hugged her sister back. Ash-ting crouched under the bed.

A few minutes later they heard the toilet flush. Then they listened as Uncle Steve's footsteps approached the doorway and he came into the room.

"Hello Mel," he whispered. "Are you awake?"

The two little girls lay still holding each other tight. Then Tara glimpsed a tiny bright light on the wall and knew it was her angel – she felt less afraid knowing her guardian angel was with them. Uncle Steve crossed the room and sat on the edge of the bed. When he realized they were both in the bed he said in a fierce voice, "Go back to your own bed immediately Tara."

Just then Jack cried out. He'd woken with a nightmare and was calling for Mummy. Uncle Steve was furious. Muttering "I'll be back," he left the room. The girls got out of bed and ran after him to comfort their little brother.

They heard Uncle Steve sound really cross because Jack had wet the bed. They heard him smack the little boy and Jack howled. No one had ever hit him before. Suddenly Tara found her voice.

She ran at the man, shouting angrily.

Mel pressed Mum's number on the mobile phone. Uncle Steve saw her and grabbed the phone from her hand. Tara screamed and screamed.

Mum and Dad come back home

They didn't hear the front door opening. Suddenly Dad's voice said, "What's going on?"

"He hit Jack," screamed Tara.

Mum rushed past Dad to hug Jack and find dry pyjamas. She didn't waste time asking for explanations.

"Out!" she shouted at Uncle Steve. "Get out of this house now!"

Daddy looked at his daughters and then at Uncle Steve. Uncle Steve saw the look on his face and ran for the stairs. He didn't even collect his things. He just rushed out into the night.

Then Mummy made hot chocolate for them all and Mummy, Daddy, Mel, Tara and Jack sat hugging and talking in the sitting room.

"You should have told us," Mummy said gently. "We knew you didn't like him very much

but we never thought…" She did not finish the sentence.

Ash-ting repeated to Tara. *"Yes, you should always tell an adult if someone touches you in a way you don't like, or makes you feel afraid."*

"I did try," murmured Tara, "but my voice got stuck, so I drew him at school instead."

"I know," said Mummy. 'We saw your teacher at Tracy's house tonight. She told me about your picture and said she was concerned. That's why we came home straight away and we were almost home when the phone rang. Good girl for phoning, Mel."

"When he slapped Jack for wetting the bed, I shouted at him to stop," Tara put in.

"Yes, we heard you when we came in," said Mummy, smiling for the first time. "That's my brave tiger." She put her arms round Tara and cuddled her.

Tara didn't tell them about the angel but she knew that she would see her guardian angel again – and she was right.

Mel Needs Help

The very next day Tara was sitting in the classroom at school looking out of the window - daydreaming as she often did – when she felt a buzz in her forehead, which always came when Ash-ting was ending her a message. *Mel needs you!*

"What's wrong?'" she thought with alarm, "What can I do?"

She felt a sudden tingling all over and there was her guardian angel again, standing right beside her. The voice was still soft, but urgent, "Tara, your sister Mel has fallen into the river. Tell the teacher and then run as fast as you can to the river. I'll guide you."

Tara didn't hesitate. She ran out of her seat shouting, "Mrs. Bright, Mel's in the river, come quickly."

Mrs. Bright shouted, "Come back Tara," and tried to stop her, but Tara dodged past and ran out of the door. Something about the look on

Tara's face made Mrs. Bright hurry after her. A few seconds later the whole class streamed out of the room and across the playing field. Half the school had seen or heard the commotion and many more people were racing towards the river.

Tara's angel was showing her the way. They had already gone through the gate onto the footpath by the river. The angel led her to the right where the water was deep. She could hear faint splashing and then she could see Mel in the water.

"Mel!" screamed Tara.

Mrs. Bright shouted, "Go and fetch help." Then she jumped in.

She did not know just how much help there was. Rather too many adults and children had followed Tara and her teacher, so there were many hands to help pull Mel out of the water once Mrs Bright had got her to the bank. One of them had also called for an ambulance.

Mel was breathing, but she had swallowed a lot of water. Tara was scared when she saw her sister. She looked very white and limp. The angel said that Mel would be alright but she must get to hospital fast.

Ash-ting buzzed her, *"Ask an angel of healing to help Mel."* So she closed her eyes and asked for an angel of healing to come quickly.

Tara was allowed to go in the ambulance with Mel and a very wet Mrs. Bright. As she sat holding Mel's hand, she saw a big green healing angel sitting by her sister's head. Then she really knew everything would be alright. Mummy and Daddy met them at the hospital and lots of praise was showered on Tara.

Mel explained what had happened. She told them how she realized she had lost her sunhat when their class was on a field trip by the river, so in the lunch break she sneaked out of the school playing fields onto the tow path to look for it.

"It had blown into the reeds so I stretched out to get it and that's when I fell in," she explained. "And I couldn't get out."

"Well you're safe now," Mummy said, holding her close. "And I think you have learnt that you must never do such a thing again. You must tell an adult if you have lost something and never wander off alone like that again."

"How did you know Mel had fallen into the river?" Dad asked Tara.

"I don't know," shrugged Tara. "I just knew."

Everyone was too tired to ask any more questions. They had also got used to strange things happening ever since Tara had got Ash-ting for her birthday, and it really didn't matter anyhow – what mattered was Mel was safe. Tara's angel smiled at her.

Asking for Help

That night in bed Tara said to Ash-ting. "I wonder if I'll ever see my angel again."

He just purred as a golden light appeared in the room.

"Hello my brave Tara," said the angel. "You did very well today."

"Thank you for telling me about Mel," replied Tara politely.

"Remember, I'm always here to help you, but you must ask," the golden being continued, "and you must play your part, too."

Tara opened her mouth rather cheekily to say she'd like an ice cream, but she knew that wasn't really the kind of thing her angel meant.

"For example if a child asks his angel to help him pass his exams but doesn't do any work, his angel won't do it!"

Tara nodded. She could see the sense of that.

"But please will you help me relax when I'm doing my reading."

"Yes I will."

Tara laughed. She felt warm and safe and loved.

"Everyone has a guardian angel Tara, but they don't always ask for help. So remember to ask for help for others, too. Then we can assist lots of people."

"Please can you help those poor people who are in hospital?"

"Thank you. As soon as you asked for that more angels of healing went to the hospital."

"Wow!" Tara was amazed at how quickly this worked! "I'm going to ask angels to help lots and lots of people."

But before she could do anymore helping that night she fell fast asleep, with her golden angel and Ash-ting watching over her.

Going Too Fast

On Saturday, Dad took them all out on their bikes. They went to the big hill where Dad made them promise not to go too fast. "It's dangerous because there are trees at the bottom," he reminded them. They all solemnly declared they would ride slowly and put their brakes on.

But Tara wanted to go faster than Mel – who had a bigger bike – so she pedalled as quickly as she could. She heard Ash-ting buzzing in her head, *"Use your brakes Tara! Use your brakes!"* She could also hear Dad shouting, "Brake Tara! Brake!" But she took no notice. Her hair was streaming in the wind and she had overtaken Mel. She felt wonderful.

Suddenly Tara realized just how fast she was going. There was a clump of trees ahead of her and she pulled on her brakes, but she had left it too late and they didn't slow her down quickly enough. "Help!" she screamed. "Angel, please help!" All at once her bike skidded and by some stroke of luck she narrowly missed a tree and

bounced and slid off the path into some long grass, which broke her fall.

Her arm and side were bruised and scraped. Thankfully Dad was so relieved Tara wasn't badly hurt, he was not cross with her. "You were so lucky to miss the tree," he said in wonder, "I still can't believe it. It's a miracle."

After Mum cleaned up Tara's cuts and scrapes, she left her to rest on the sofa with a glass of juice and a biscuit. She had a big fluffy blanket over her and Ash-ting was tucked beneath it purring contentedly.

Once again the golden light began to grow beside her and her guardian angel appeared, sitting alongside her on the sofa.

"Hello Tara," she smiled gently. "How are you feeling?"

"Alright," she murmured.

"I held you as you fell, so that you missed the tree," said the angel.

"But why didn't you stop me getting hurt?" Tara wanted to know.

"I lifted you gently into that long grass, but I couldn't stop you from getting hurt because you would not have learnt your lesson. You had been told not to cycle so fast down the hill, but you didn't listen. It is important to listen to your parents and do what they say."

Tara hung her head for a moment, but her angel looked at her with such love that she was soon smiling again.

"Remember Tara," she said. "There's nothing you can do or say that will stop me from loving you."

The Unhappy Dog

When Mum collected the children from school on Monday, Tara was very excited. Her teacher had decided to change Tara's reading programme and she had really enjoyed today's special lesson.

"I think I will soon be reading just fine Mum", said Tara with a huge smile on her face. She didn't tell her Mum how she had asked her angel to help her, and how a soft golden warm energy had surrounded her in the classroom, helping her to relax and concentrate.

Mum hugged Tara and wondered what kind of miracle had occurred for her little girl to suddenly be so happy about reading. They held hands and set off for home with a spring in their steps.

At the end of their road they passed by a very dingy house with long uncut grass and weeds in the front. Sometimes they could hear a dog howling inside and once they saw it scratching at a window and barking. "It's not right," said her

Mum every time they passed it. "Someone should do something about that poor dog." But no one ever did.

That morning they had heard a man shout at the dog to be quiet and then they heard it whimper. Quietly Tara asked the angel of animals to please help the dog. At lunchtime she repeated her request and asked that the dog be taken somewhere where he could be happy and safe.

As they passed by the house on the way home from school they saw a nice-looking elderly lady park her car outside the house.

"Are you coming to take the dog?" Tara asked her.

"Hush Tara," said Mummy. "It's none of our business."

But the lady stared at Tara in astonishment. "How did you know? He was my daughter's dog and since she's been ill my son-in-law can't cope with him. He phoned me up at lunch time and said the idea had just popped into his head to ask me to look after him."

"Thank you angels," whispered a smiling Tara. She knew where the idea had come from.

They watched as the lady opened the front door and brought out a bouncy energetic terrier. He clearly knew the lady and loved her.

"I've got a big garden and I'll love taking him for walks," she told them as she got back into the car again.

The dog looked at Tara and gave one short sharp bark. She knew he was saying thank you for asking the angels to help.

Tara loves asking the angels to help people and watching them move into action straight away.

Whenever Tara sees an ambulance she asks angels of healing to help the patient inside it and she immediately sees lovely green healing angels flying with the vehicle.

When she passes someone who looks sad, she asks angels of love to touch them and watches the angels surround them with love and light.

She often asks her angel to help her too and is no longer surprised when things just work out ok.

Tara, Ash-ting and the Fairies

Tara and her fluffy grey kitten, Ash-ting, lay cuddled together in a cosy sleeping bag. They were staring out of the tent flap at a beautiful big, shiny full moon. It was the middle of the night but almost as light as day, though the shadows were very dark.

Tara's little brother Jack was staying at Granny's and her big sister Mel had a sleep over at a friend's, so Daddy said he'd pitch the tent in the garden and he and Tara could sleep in it for a special treat. Tara loved the thrill of sleeping outdoors. Her Daddy was fast asleep and snoring and she was wide awake.

Tara and Ash-ting looked at each other and smiled. They had a wonderful secret that no one else knew. They could talk to each other!

"I'd love to play outside," whispered Tara.

"Come on then. The fairies and elves are under the oak tree."

"Fairies and elves! Are they real?" exclaimed Tara.

"Of course," chuckled Ash-ting, *"without them the flowers and vegetables and trees wouldn't grow."*

'Oh!' mouthed the little girl in surprise as she crept out of her sleeping bag and tiptoed onto the lawn. The child and the kitten walked in the silver river of bright moonlight to the end of the garden, where a path led onto a meadow in which stood a huge old oak tree. And sure enough, under the tree there sat a row of little people, all looking at her. Tara could hardly believe her eyes.

"Meow," called Ash-ting in greeting. They all jumped for they were so intent on watching Tara they had not seen him. Then they waved and shouted greetings.

"Hello Ash-ting. Is this Tara?"

"Yes, this is my friend Tara," the kitten replied. Suddenly Tara felt very shy as Ash-ting introduced her to fairies, elves, pixies, gnomes, imps and brownies. They clustered round her in excitement and one tiny imp flew onto the palm of her hand. She held him up close to her face and laughed as he danced and tickled her hand. "I'm Ivan," he grinned and Tara grinned back.

A bright pink fairy called Rose took her hand.

"How come I can see you and talk to you?" Tara gasped.

Rose explained how when you want to watch something on television you tune into the right channel, and then you can see and hear your programme.

"It's the same with us," she chuckled

cheerfully. "When you are ready to meet us, you automatically tune into our wavelength."

"And I am ready?"

"Yes. You read books about us, draw pictures of us and you love the trees and flowers we work with. And you have learnt much from Ash-ting."

'Wow!' laughed the little girl.

Two elves dressed in green with pointed green hats jumped forwards to introduce themselves. "I'm Leafy", bowed one "and I am Elveera," bowed the other. Their voices sounded like the wind in the trees.

A group of pixies, who were taller and thinner than the elves, were standing together. "Pleased to meet you Tara and Ash-ting, we're just visiting this area. We travel where we are needed to help the soil."

"Hello," she replied. "I wish you'd help my Daddy with the soil in his allotment. He says it's too sandy."

The pixies nodded and agreed to see what they could do.

The Caterpillar

Despite their cheery greetings, most of the little people looked quite glum.

"Why do they all look so sad?" Tara whispered to Ash-ting.

"Because of the oak tree," the kitten replied, *"people are going to chop it down and put a road through here."*

'No!' exclaimed Tara. 'They can't chop down the oak tree.'

She looked up at the huge branches of the tree she had known and loved all her life. She knew the tree was very old indeed.

"And they'll cut down the beech wood over there." He looked towards the copse to the right of the meadow.

"That's terrible," she shook her head; "they can't do that."

"They can," said the elves gloomily.

"Ash-ting will know what to do, won't you?" she begged the kitten. But he shook his head.

"It's all going ahead. They are starting the day after tomorrow. There's nothing we can do."

Tara was shocked because usually Ash-ting found a solution.

Suddenly Tara noticed a black caterpillar with a yellow line down it. Two little elfin creatures with pointed wings were stroking it. One went to its head and urged it to move. "You're in the middle of the path and a bird will eat you. Move!" she urged. The caterpillar lifted its head and wriggled a little, but he was too tired and flopped down again. The little elemental sighed.

"Who are you?" Tara asked.

"We're brownies. We help the elves and trees, and insects and animals too." they answered.

The brownies turned back to the caterpillar and stroked it again. "Go on, get into some

shelter," but the weary caterpillar just lay there.

"It will be a beautiful red admiral butterfly when it grows up," said one of the brownies. Then she added sadly, "If it grows up. We can try to help it but we can't budge it."

"But I can," exclaimed Tara. She found a large leaf which she pushed very gently under the caterpillar.

"Put him amongst the stinging nettles, red admiral caterpillars love to eat them," encouraged the brownies.

Tara placed him gently among the nettles and the brownies and elves clapped, their eyes shining with gratitude.

"Thank you so much Tara," they sang in unison. The child glowed with pleasure and Ash-ting gave her a meow of thanks too.

The Oak Tree

Suddenly everyone fell silent as they heard the tree give a loud creak. All the little folk stood up respectfully. Tara wondered what was happening. Then she stared in amazement as she saw a face begin to appear in the trunk of the tree. It was a very old face and yet its eyes were shining and full of life.

Ash-ting explained that it was the guardian of the tree, who was a very knowledgeable and wise being. He told her how the guardian holds the energy and all the history of the area and helps to protect it.

She watched as the tree spirit stepped out of the tree and stood in front of her. At first it was enormously tall then it became smaller so it was the height of a person. The guardian radiated such peace and kindness that she was quite unafraid. She could understand why the elves lived in its branches.

"Once this whole county was a huge forest," the spirit said. 'Now there are few trees left and

we have to do the work that they all did. It really helps us when you humans appreciate us." Then he vanished.

Tara put her arms round the big oak and hugged it.

"Thank you for everything, I wish I could help you."

Going Back to the Tent

One of the elves was angry. "Why should we help humans when they do these terrible things to our trees!" he shouted. Several others jumped up and down in rage and Tara felt alarmed. A beautiful pink fairy flew over and took Tara's hand. "Don't be scared, they are just afraid and upset," she said. "They won't harm you."

"It's time to go back to the tent now," said Ash-ting firmly, looking up at the sky.

At that moment a big black cloud blotted out the moon. In an instant it was pitch dark.

"Oh," squeaked Tara. "Ash-ting, where are you?"

"Here I am," he replied rubbing against her legs.

"We'll guide you back," said the fairies and a dozen of them, like beautiful coloured lights, lit the way. "This is amazing," thought the little girl as Ash-ting with his tail in the air marched in front and all the fairies danced round her. "It's like magic."

In the morning Tara asked Daddy about the oak tree. He sighed.

"They're going to build a by-pass round the village. I'm afraid the oak tree will come down and the trees in the wood. It's very sad."

"Ask him what can be done to stop it," urged Ash-ting.

"Can anything be done to help the tree, Daddy?"

"No. We've done all we can. They are starting work the day after tomorrow. I'm afraid we'll lose the oak, the meadow and the woods."

Mummy came out with their breakfast and heard their conversation.

"I wish they could find a rare animal there. That would save it," she said, giving Dad a cup of tea and Tara a glass of juice.

"How was your night in the tent, Tara?"

Ash-ting gave her a warning look.

"It was lovely thank you Mummy. Can we please sleep in the tent again tonight?"

Dad looked at Mum.

"Well, it's probably the last chance before the noise and dust of the road works starts."

"Okay. But Jack will have to join you. He's coming home from Granny's this afternoon."

Tara felt angry. She wanted to protest but Ash-ting told her to smile and say thank you, so she did. Later she grumbled to Ash-ting. "Jack will spoil everything."

"No, he'll be fast asleep. And Tara I have an idea!"

Endangered species.

Water vole
Greater horseshoe bat
Field cricket
Dormouse
Red squirrel

Endangered Animals

Dad was surprised and pleased to see Tara taking such a sudden interest in endangered animals, especially those that are protected. They went onto the internet together and she looked very carefully at all the pictures and asked lots of question. Dad even helped her write down some names. Ash-ting sat beside her and nodded wisely.

That afternoon she cycled to the allotment with Daddy. Usually she hated going and said it was boring, but today was different. She wondered if the pixies would be there and she would so like to see the fairies again. And sure enough, when they arrived she could see fairies, elves, brownies, imps, gnomes and a whole host of little spirits busy at work amongst the flowers and vegetables.

The pixies were there, too. They were in the compost heap, but she couldn't quite see what they were doing. They all stopped and smiled when they saw her. "Hello Tara, have you come to help us then?"

"What can I do?"

"Talk to the vegetables and picture them growing huge! Or sing to them, because they love pretty music" said one of the elves and all the others nodded.

"You don't just look after them physically. You must encourage them in every way."

"OK," agreed Tara and wondered what her friends would say if they could see her singing to the plants.

Daddy looked round as he heard his little girl singing beautifully while looking at a row of cabbages. He looked around his plot and scratched his head.

"I don't know what it is, but everything looks a bit different today," he said

"It's because I'm here," she replied laughing.

Ash-ting's Plan

That night Tara fell fast asleep as soon as she got into her sleeping bag. Ash-ting had to pat her face to wake her up. The first thing she saw was Rose, the bright pink fairy, with a yellow one called Sunflower and a beautiful blue one called Delphinium, who were peeping round the opening in the tent.

Without waking Jack or Daddy, she and Ash-ting crept out of her sleeping bag and followed their fairy friends outside. Tara smiled with delight as Rose landed on her shoulder and sat there swinging her legs.

A huge crowd of gloomy looking pixies, elves, imps and brownies were waiting for them under the oak tree and they all sat down to talk. Ash-ting told them his plan. Everyone was excited. Tara read out her list of endangered animals and insects. The guardian of the oak tree was delighted.

"I'll send a message through the tree network

for all these creatures to come out of hiding," he boomed.

"You and Ash-ting stay here," commanded Rose. "We'll search for them and bring them here. If we need you, we'll call you. But first we must tell everyone what is happening."

She started to sing a beautiful melody and then everyone joined in. Tara and Ash-ting could hear a wonderful hum rising up all round them and it seemed to get bigger and bigger, as if thousands of elementals were joining in. It travelled for miles.

Soon Tara and Ash-ting were alone with the tree. Tara hugged her kitten close and felt a little impatient, but she knew she must do as she was told and wait here. She could see down the path into her garden where Daddy and Jack were still fast asleep in the tent. She felt very excited.

And then they saw an amazing sight. A column of rarely seen creatures was winding its way towards the tree. With them were hundreds of fairies, elves, imps and pixies.

A wrinkled old toad was crawling slowly, encouraged by two pixies. Dozens of beetles were scuttling together with cheerful imps riding on their backs, the moonlight shimmering in different colours on their hard cases. Glow worms were flashing on and off.

Then there were hosts of brownies pulling leaves on which sat all sorts of unusual insects. It took several elves to drag a sleeping dormouse on a piece of bark, while a nervous water vole was being gently stroked by a fairy to give it courage to continue.

Several lizards were running backwards and forwards excitedly urging the others on. Rare crickets chirruped as they leapt along the path, sometimes landing on another insect but everyone was in a good mood, so they didn't mind.

At the back three big slow tortoises carried hundreds of creatures who couldn't get to the tree by themselves.

And above the column flew rare moths and flying bugs, while fairies directed the way.

When they reached the tree the cavalcade hid in the roots, climbed into holes in the trunk, crept behind the bark, wriggled behind the leaves

or nestled or perched on the branches.

Then a pair of rare birds landed on the top branches. By the light of the moon they set about building a nest and the fairies helped them, flying up with twigs and moss that Tara was busy gathering.

The oak tree was always full of insects and small animals. But now it was more alive with them than ever before. Now it was humming, chirping, singing and buzzing with them. All the little people celebrated and Tara and Ash-ting sat among a thousand nature spirits all singing joyfully.

It was truly a night to remember, but it was also time for Tara and Ash-ting to return to their tent.

Next Morning

Early next morning Ash-ting jumped on Tara to wake her up.

"Come on Tara, get up. Ask your Dad to come to the tree one last time."

She pulled on her clothes as she shouted to Daddy.

"Come on Daddy, can we please go to see the oak tree one last time?"

"Okay," he said, but his eyes looked very sad.

"But can't it wait till after breakfast?" he asked.

"No Daddy. Please can we go now?"

She looked so insistent that he picked up Jack, who was still in his pyjamas, and they hurried off to the tree together.

The men with the diggers and chain saws were just arriving. One of them tried to wave them back but Dad said gently that they had come to say goodbye to the tree. The man shrugged and turned away. Then Dad's eyes opened wide. He saw a rare beetle, an almost extinct vole, a lizard, a dormouse and a frog. He didn't see the little faces peeping down at him from between the leaves though – but Tara did.

Tara's Dad immediately pulled out his phone and made lots of urgent phone calls. Before very long there were cars full of people pulling up at the edge of the meadow. The press arrived, wildlife experts, the police, a helicopter and lots of local people. The road contractors were protesting, they wanted to get on with their job and were getting very red faced and angry.

"No one's going to cut down that tree or build a road now," said Dad happily. And he was right.

The Admiral Butterfly

A week or so later when all the fuss had died down Tara tried to tell Mum about fairies and elves.

"You have to be able to tune into their wavelength," she explained.

"You always did have a good imagination Tara," laughed her Mum.

Tara felt a bit frustrated, it WASN'T her imagination! Just then a beautiful red admiral butterfly landed on Tara's arm and spread out its colourful wings.

"Thank you Tara for saving me," it whispered, before flying away again.

Tara and Ash-ting watched it go and grinned at each other.

In the same collection...

The Magical Adventures of Tara and the Talking Kitten

By Diana Cooper

Illustrated by Kate Shannon

and more to come!